Matthew and the Bullies

By Sarah, Duchess of York

Illustrated by Ian Cunliffe

STERLING

New York / London

STERLING and the distinctive Sterling logo are registered trademarks of
Sterling Publishing Co., Inc.

Library of Congress Cataloging-in-Publication Data

York, Sarah Mountbatten-Windsor, Duchess of, 1959-
[Charlie and the bullies]
Matthew and the bullies / by Sarah, Duchess of York ; illustrated by Ian Cunliffe.
p. cm. -- (Helping hand)
Summary: Matthew learns how to deal with the bullies at his school the proper way--by
asking his parents and teacher for help. Includes note to parents.
ISBN 978-1-4027-7391-4
[1. Bullies--Fiction. 2. Schools--Fiction.] I. Cunliffe, Ian, ill. II. Title.
PZ7.Y823Mat 2010
[E]--dc22
2009042178

Lot #:
2 4 6 8 10 9 7 5 3
06/10
Published by Sterling Publishing Co., Inc.
387 Park Avenue South, New York, NY 10016
Story and illustrations © 2007 by Startworks Ltd
'Ten Helpful Hints' © 2009 by Startworks Ltd
Distributed in Canada by Sterling Publishing
c/o Canadian Manda Group, 165 Dufferin Street
Toronto, Ontario, Canada M6K 3H6
Distributed in Australia by Capricorn Link (Australia) Pty. Ltd.
P.O. Box 704, Windsor, NSW 2756, Australia

Sterling ISBN 978-1-4027-7391-4

For information about custom editions, special sales, premium and
corporate purchases, please contact Sterling Special Sales
Department at 800-805-5489 or specialsales@sterlingpublishing.com.

All children face many new experiences as they grow up, and helping them to understand and deal with each is one of the most demanding and rewarding things we do as parents. Helping Hand Books are for both children and parents to read, perhaps together. Each simple story describes a childhood experience and shows some of the ways in which to make it a positive one. I do hope these books encourage children and parents to talk about these sometimes difficult issues. Talking together goes a long way to finding a solution.

Sarah,

Sarah, Duchess of York

Matthew felt sick every morning as he got ready for school. It wasn't the schoolwork that worried him. It was the time when he wasn't in class, particularly recess. Matthew was small for his age, and although he could run very fast, some of the boys were bigger and they teased Matthew whenever they saw him.

Over time, the teasing got worse and turned to pushing and shoving. One day during recess, John, one of the boys in Matthew's class, pushed him against a wall. Matthew wanted to fight back, but he knew it would only make things worse.

That evening, Matthew's mom saw his scraped knees and bruises and asked him how he got them.

"We were playing around at recess," said Matthew, not completely truthfully, "and I fell over."

"Try to be more careful," said his mom. "You only have the one body."

Matthew desperately wanted to tell his mom the real reason for the scrapes and bruises, but he worried he would get into even more trouble if he did. He thought it was his fault that the other boys didn't like him and wanted to solve the problem on his own.

The next morning, Matthew was really scared, but he said nothing and went to school. For the next few days, Matthew spent as much time as possible playing with lots of other kids so that he was always in a group. But when John and his friend Daniel found Matthew alone, they started to push and tease him again.

Because he could run fast, Matthew ducked between them and ran into the classroom. But there he put his head in his hands and sobbed.

A few minutes later, the door opened and in came Amy, who sat down next to Matthew.

"Hi, Matthew!" said Amy, but Matthew did not reply. "You've been crying!" she said.

"You would too if you were me," said Matthew sadly.

Matthew told Amy all about the bullies. "And I'm supposed to give my show-and-tell presentation this week, but now I'm too scared to stand up in front of the class," he added.

"You have to tell your mom and dad," said Amy.

"They wouldn't understand," said Matthew.

"Then I think you should tell Mrs. Watson," Amy replied.

"Tell me what?" said a voice behind them.

They both turned to see Mrs. Watson, their teacher, standing at the door.

"Nothing," said Matthew quickly, "nothing at all," and glared at Amy.

That evening, Matthew thought about what Amy had said. He thought maybe his mom would understand.

"Mom," he said as he was eating his dinner, "can I tell you something?"

"Of course," said his mom. "You know you can tell Dad and me anything."

Matthew told the whole story to his mom. When he was finished, he cried, not because he was sad but because he was so relieved to have shared his problem. As his mom comforted him, she said, "I wish you had told me sooner, but together we can solve this."

"I think I should fight back,"
said Matthew.

"No, you should not!" replied his mom.
"You would be acting just as badly as they are."

They talked for a long time and finally his mom said,
"You will have to let me tell Mrs. Watson."

Matthew was upset at first but then he decided to trust his
mom and his teacher. He knew it was the right thing to do.

The next morning was the day of Matthew's show-and-tell presentation, and he did not feel so brave. He told his mom he wasn't going to school.

"Yes, you are," said his mom. "It's your big day. You don't have to be nervous because your presentation is going to be great. I spoke with Mrs. Watson last night. She called John and Daniel's parents and will be speaking with the boys today."

Before class, Mrs. Watson explained to John and Daniel that bullying was not tolerated in their school. She asked them why they kept bothering Matthew so much. They had no answer. Suddenly, they felt embarrassed for being mean to someone who had never harmed them.

"You did the right thing in telling someone," Mrs. Watson told Matthew. "Now, I can't wait to hear your show-and-tell presentation."

Matthew walked up to the front of the class. With a nervous smile, he looked at John and Daniel sitting at their desks. Matthew remembered to be brave and started his presentation. He showed the class a poster he had made of all his sports awards—for swimming, running, baseball, and especially soccer. The class had no idea Matthew was such a good athlete.

When it was time to go home that afternoon, John and Daniel were waiting outside the school. Matthew was so excited about his presentation that he barely even noticed them.

"Don't worry," said John. "We're going to leave you alone from now on."

"That works for me," said Matthew, "but I was kind of hoping you'd play soccer with me this weekend."

"Really?" said John.

"Sure," answered Matthew with a smile. "I could really use some more practice."

The three boys smiled.

And that is how a brave boy turned two bullies into two friends.

TEN HELPFUL HINTS

FOR PARENTS WHOSE CHILD IS BEING BULLIED

By Dr. Richard Woolfson, PhD

1. Always treat complaints of bullying seriously. Remember that it takes a great deal of courage for your child to admit to you that she is being bullied. Reassure her that you will deal with things carefully and tactfully.

2. Let your child know that you understand how difficult this is for him to cope with. He needs to feel that you don't think badly of him for complaining.

3. Emphasize that this is now a shared problem which can be solved. Tell your child that that you and she will work together on this until the bullying stops.

4. Boost your child's self-confidence. Help him feel more positively about himself and his achievements. Remind him of all his strong skills and emphasize that you think he is wonderful.

5. Persuade your child to walk away discreetly whenever the bully appears to be moving in her direction. Make her aware that this is not an act of cowardice.

6. Tell your child not to react when confronted by a bully. Ignoring verbal and physical threats is difficult, but the bully will stop eventually if he gets no reaction.

7.   Don't tell your child to fight back. Even if he succeeds, he will think this is an acceptable way of dealing with all sorts of problems in his life.

8.   Suggest your child stays in a crowd, especially in free time such as recess. Bullies pick on children who seem weak and isolated. A child standing alone in the school playground is easily identified as a potential target.

9.   Encourage your child to look assertive and walk with confidence, especially near a bully. Looking directly ahead rather than towards the ground will project a strong image.

10. Speak to school staff and insist that the school take a zero-tolerance policy towards bullying. Bullying is most effectively tackled in collaboration with teachers, parents, and pupils. Explain to the teacher that your child is worried about being centered out for complaining, and work out a plan to make sure your child is protected in school.

Dr. Richard Woolfson is a child psychologist, working with children and their families. He is also an author and has written several books on child development and family life, in addition to numerous articles for magazines and newspapers. Dr. Woolfson runs training workshops for parents and child care professionals and appears regularly on radio and television. He is a Fellow of the British Psychological Society.

Helping Hand Books

Look for these other helpful books to share with your child: